THE
TREASURE
SELMA LAGERLÖF

DAUGHTERS, INC.

Plainfield, Vermont

ISBN: 0-913780-01-4
Library of Congress Catalog Card Number: 73-86275

Manufactured in the United States of America

Second Printing

Designed by Loretta Li

THE
TREASURE

FOREWORD

*Because the Foreword reveals the book's ending, we suggest that you read the story first.

The Treasure is an opposite fairy tale, presenting Prince Charming as he really is: an orphan girl is cleaning fish and foreseeing her life of poverty; a man well-dressed in seductive splendor woos her and offers her . . . foreverafter. There is only one catch: she must betray her sister.

Although Selma Lagerlöf won the Nobel Prize for literature in 1909, her name is known in this country— if at all—as author of a children's book only. All her other works, including novels and feminist essays, have been unavailable in English for almost fifty years.

In 1911, she made a speech entitled "Home and State" to the International Woman Suffrage Alliance

v

Congress. She argued, first, that the Home was the creation of woman and the place where the values of women were nourished and protected. The Home was a community where "punishment is not for the sake of revenge, but for training and education," where "there is a use for all talents, but [she] who is without can make [her]self as much loved as the cleverest." It was the "storehouse for the songs and legends of our forefathers," and, she said, "there is nothing more mobile, more merciful amongst the creations of [humankind]." Although not all homes are good, good and happy homes do sometimes exist.

Men by themselves, on the other hand, were responsible for creating the State which "continually gives cause for discontent and bitterness." There has never been a State which could satisfy all its members, which did not ask to be reformed from its very foundations. Yet it is through the State that humankind will reach its highest hopes. Her conclusion: women must add their special virtues, what she calls "God's spirit," to the "law and order" goals of men.

Selma Lagerlöf's own home was a community of family and servants, within which she experienced profound affections—for the nursemaid who carried her as a crippled child upon her back, for the old housekeeper, her younger sister, her grandmother who told the children stories every afternoon. She never married; she spent her entire life within communities of women, and her career could be described as the author being handed up to greatness by a procession of women who gave encouragement, advice, editorial help, criticism, contacts, companionship. She called Frederika Bremer the first feminist and "last old Mamsell" of Sweden, meaning that Frederika Bremer's life's work had banished the "old maid" from the realm of pitiful figures. Selma Lagerlöf was herself proof of her statement.

In *The Treasure*, written midway between her farewell to Frederika Bremer and her plea for woman suffrage, the men are interested in money, murder, and revenge. They miss the evil apparent even to their dogs. When the old mistress (and who should know better that the home is threatened?) warns that knives are being sharpened two miles away, her lord refuses to believe that she could hear what he cannot. The fishpeddler's dog has instinct enough to balk and howl, sensing death; the fishpeddler's wife and the woman tavern-keeper respond to the supernatural however little they understand; the men turn their backs on understanding even when they are being implored.

But the thrust of the story deals with the maiden Elsalill's painful struggle to choose between her dearest sister, who has had to wander so long on earth "she has worn her feet to bleeding" and can find grave's rest only if her murderer is apprehended; and Sir Archie, the murderer himself, whom Elsalill loves with all her heart.

Sir Archie is a subtle Prince Charming; he understands innocence and tempts Elsalill mightily: "You are a poor orphan, so forlorn and friendless that none will care what becomes of you. But if you come with me, I will make you a noble lady. I am a powerful man in my own country. You shall be clad in silk and gold, and you shall tread a measure at the King's court."

Even after Elsalill knows that her love is the murderer of her sister, she still hopes to escape the action this knowledge demands: she tries to persuade herself that because he wants to make up to Elsalill for the evil he did to her sister, she should give him a chance to save his soul. She thinks that her sister does not know he will atone for his sin and become a good man; her sister could not wish her unhappiness; how can she ask that Elsalill betray the man she loves?

But she hears her sister weep and she sees her sister's blood on the snow, and she turns him in quickly, hoping that will be enough. It isn't. Her choice requires that she give her life.

At the book's end Sir Archie, still clinging to his be-lief in money-power, still trying to use her saintliness to save his own soul, says he will erect a grand monument to her memory. He believes that if he leaves her body in Marstand she will have only a pauper's grave and be soon forgotten. An exactly opposite event occurs. A long procession walks out across the ice toward the ship; all the women of Marstand, young and old, are coming to retrieve Elsalill's body and carry her back "with all the honor that is her due."

The Treasure is a fable, a fairytale, an allegory of sisterhood itself. There is good reason that this book has been out of print for two generations. Daughters, Inc. is proud to retrieve Selma Lagerlöf and publish her in English once again—with all the honor that is her due.

June Arnold

Plainfield, Vermont
1973

I

In the days when King Frederik the Second of Denmark ruled over Bohuslen there dwelt at Marstrand a poor hawker of fish, whose name was Torarin. This man was infirm and of humble condition; he had a palsied arm, which made him unfit to take his place in a boat for fishing or pulling an oar. As he could not earn his livelihood at sea like all the other men of the skerries, he went about selling salted and dried fish among the people of the mainland. Not many days in the year did he spend at home; he was constantly on the road from one village to another with his load of fish.

One February day, as dusk was drawing on, Torarin came driving along the road which led from Kungshall up to the parish of Solberga. The road was a lonely one, altogether deserted, but this was no reason for Torarin to hold his tongue. Beside him on the sledge he had a trusty friend with whom to chat. This was a little black dog with shaggy coat, and Torarin called him Grim. He lay still most of the time, with his head sunk between his feet, and answered only by blinking to all his master said. But if his ear caught anything that displeased him, he stood up on the load, put his nose in the air, and howled worse than a wolf.

"Now I must tell you, Grim, my dog," said Torarin, "that I have heard great news today. They told me both at Kungshall and at Kareby that the sea was frozen. Fair, calm weather it has been this long while, as you well know, who have been out in it every day; and they say the sea is frozen fast not only in the creeks and sounds, but far out over the Cattegat. There is no fairway now for ship or boat among the islands, nothing but firm, hard ice, so that a man may drive with horse and sledge as far as Marstrand and Paternoster Skerries."

To all this the dog listened, and it seemed not to displease him. He lay still and blinked at Torarin.

"We have no great store of fish left on our load," said Torarin, as though trying to talk him over. "What would you say to turning aside at the next crossways and going westward where the sea lies? We shall pass by Solberga church and down to Odsmalskil, and after that I think we have but seven or eight miles to Marstrand. It would be a fine thing if we could reach home for once without calling for boat or ferry."

They drove on over the long moor of Kareby, and although the weather had been calm all day, a chill breeze came sweeping across the moor, to the discomfort of the traveller.

"It may seem like softness to go home now when trade is at its best," said Torarin, flinging out his arms to warm them. "But we have been on the road for many weeks, you and I, and have a claim to sit at home a day or two and thaw the cold out of our bodies."

As the dog continued to lie still, Torarin seemed to grow more sure of his ground, and he went on in a more cheerful tone:

"Mother has been left alone in the cottage these many days. I warrant she longs to see us. And Marstrand is a fine town in wintertime, Grim, with streets and alleys full of foreign fishermen and chapmen. There will be dancing in the wharves every night of the week. And all the ale that will be flowing in the taverns! That is a thing beyond your understanding."

As Torarin said this he bent down over the dog to see whether he was listening to what was said to him.

But as the dog lay there wide awake and made no sign of displeasure, Torarin turned off at the first road that led westward to the sea. He flicked the horse with the slack of the reins and made it quicken its pace.

"Since we shall pass by Solberga parsonage," said Torarin, "I will even put in there and ask if it be true that the ice bears as far as to Marstrand. The folk there must know how it is."

Torarin had said these words in a low voice, without thinking whether the dog was listening or not. But scarcely were the words uttered when the dog stood up on the load and raised a terrible howl.

The horse made a bound to one side, and Torarin himself was startled and looked about him to see whether wolves were in pursuit. But when he found it was Grim who was howling, he tried to calm him.

"What now?" he said to him. "How many times have you and I driven into the parson's yard at Solberga! I know not whether Herr Arne can tell us how it is with the ice, but I will be bound he'll give us a good supper before we set out on our sea voyage."

But his words were not able to quiet the dog, who raised his muzzle and howled more dismally than ever.

At this Torarin himself was not far from yielding to an uncanny feeling. It had now grown almost dark, but still Torarin could see Solberga church and the wide plain around it, which was sheltered by broad wooded heights to landward and by bare, rounded rocks toward the sea. As he drove on in solitude over the vast white plain, he felt he was a wretched little worm, while from the dark forests and the mountain wastes came troops of great monsters and trolls of every kind venturing into the open country on the fall of darkness. And in the whole great plain there was none other for them to fall upon than poor Torarin.

But at the same time he tried again to quiet the dog.

"Bless me, what is your quarrel with Herr Arne? He is the richest man in the country. He is of noble birth, and had he not been a priest there would have been a great lord of him."

But this could not avail to bring the dog to silence. Then Torarin lost patience, so that he took Grim by the scruff of the neck and threw him off the sledge.

The dog did not follow him as he drove on, but stood still upon the road and howled without ceasing until Torarin drove under a dark archway into the yard of the parsonage, which was surrounded on its four sides by long, low wooden buildings.

At Solberga parsonage the priest, Herr Arne, sat at supper surrounded by all his household. There was no stranger present but Torarin.

Herr Arne was an old white-haired man, but he was still powerful and erect. His wife sat beside him. To her the years had been unkind; her head and her hands trembled, and she was nearly deaf. On Herr Arne's other side sat his curate. He was a pale young man with a look of trouble in his face, as though he was unable to support all the learning he had gathered in during his years of study at Wittenberg.

These three sat at the head of the table, a little apart from the rest. Below them sat Torarin, and then the servants, who were old like their master. There were three serving-men; their heads were bald, their backs bent, and their eyes blinked and watered. Of women there were but two. They were somewhat younger and more able-bodied than the men, yet they too had a fragile look

look and were afflicted with the infirmities of age.

At the farthest end of the table sat two children. One of them was Herr Arne's niece, a child of no more than fourteen years. She was fair-haired and of delicate build; her face had not yet reached its fullness, but had a promise of beauty in it. She had another little maid sitting beside her, a poor orphan without father or mother, who had been given a home at the parsonage. The two sat close together on the bench, and it could be seen that there was great friendship between them.

All these folk sat at meat in the deepest silence. Torarin looked from one to another, but none was disposed to talk during the meal. All the old servants thought to themselves: "It is a goodly thing to be given food and to be spared the sufferings of want and hunger, which we have known so often in our lives. While we are eating we ought to have no thought but of giving thanks to God for His goodness."

Since Torarin found no one to talk to, his glance wandered up and down the room. He turned his eyes from the great stove, built up in many stages beside the entrance door, to the lofty four-post bed which stood in the farthest corner of the room. He looked from the fixed benches that ran round the room to the hole in the roof, through which the smoke escaped and wintry air poured in.

As Torarin the fish hawker, who lived in the smallest and poorest cabin on the outer isles, looked upon all these things, he thought: "Were I a great man like Herr Arne I would not be content to live in an ancient homestead with only one room. I should build myself a house with high gables and many chambers, like those of the burgo-masters and aldermen of Marstrand."

But more often than not Torarin's eyes rested upon a great oaken chest which stood at the foot of the four-post bed. And he looked at it so long because he knew that in it Herr Arne kept all his silver moneys, and he had heard they were so many that they filled the chest to the very lid.

And Torarin, who was so poor that he hardly ever had a silver piece in his pocket, said to himself: "And yet I would not have

11

all that money. They say Herr Arne took it from the great convents that were in the land in former days, and that the old monks foretold that this money would bring him misfortune."

While yet these thoughts were in the mind of Torarin, he saw the old mistress of the house put her hand to her ear to listen. And then she turned to Herr Arne and asked him: "Why are they whetting knives at Branehog?"

So deep was the silence in the room that when the old lady asked this question all gave a start and looked up in fright. When they saw that she was listening for something, they kept their spoons quiet and strained their ears.

For some moments there was dead stillness in the room, but while it lasted the old woman became more and more uneasy. She laid her hand on Herr Arne's arm and asked him: "How can it be that they are whetting such long knives at Branehog this evening?"

Torarin saw that Herr Arne stroked her hand to calm her. But he was in no mind to answer and ate on calmly as before.

The old woman still sat listening. Tears

came into her eyes from terror, and her hands and her head trembled more and more violently.

Then the two little maids who sat at the end of the table began to weep with fear.

"Can you not hear them scraping and filing?" asked the old mistress. "Can you not hear them hissing and grating?"

Herr Arne sat still, stroking his wife's hand. As long as he kept silence no other dared utter a word.

But they were all assured that their old mistress had heard a thing that was terrifying and boded ill. All felt the blood curdling in their veins. No one at the table raised a bit of food to his mouth, except old Herr Arne himself.

They were thinking of the old mistress, how it was she who for so many years had had charge of the household. She had always stayed at home and watched with wise and tender care over children and servants, goods and cattle, so that all had prospered. Now she was worn out and stricken in years, but still it was likely that she and none other should feel a danger that threatened the house.

The old lady grew more and more terrified. She clasped her hands in her helplessness and began to weep so sorely that the big tears ran down her shrunken cheeks.

"Is it nothing to you, Arne Arneson, that I am so sore afraid?" she complained.

Herr Arne bent his head to her and said: "I know not what it is that affrights you."

"I am in fear of the long knives they are whetting at Branehog," she said.

"How can you hear them whetting knives at Branehog?" said Herr Arne, smiling. "The place lies two miles from here. Take up your spoon again and let us finish our supper."

The old woman made an effort to overcome her terror. She took up her spoon and dipped it in the milk bowl, but in doing it her hand shook so that all could hear the spoon rattle against the edge. She put it down again at once. "How can I eat?" she said. "Do I not hear the whining of the whetstone, do I not hear it grating?"

At this Herr Arne thrust the milk bowl away from him and clasped his hands. All the others did the same, and the curate began to say grace.

When this was ended, Herr Arne looked down at those who sat along the table, and when he saw that they were pale and frightened, he was angry.

He began to speak to them of the days when he had lately come to Bohuslen to preach the Lutheran doctrine. Then he and his servants were forced to fly from the Papists like wild beasts before the hunter. "Have we not seen our enemies lie in wait for us as we were on our way to the house of God? Have we not been driven out of the parsonage, and have we not been compelled to take to the woods like outlaws? Does it beseem us to play the coward and give ourselves up for lost on account of an evil omen?"

As Herr Arne said this he looked like a valiant champion, and the others took heart anew on hearing him.

"Ay, it is true," they thought. "God has protected Herr Arne through the greatest perils. He holds His hand over him. He will not let His servant perish."

As soon as Torarin drove out upon the road his dog Grim came up to him and jumped up on to the load. When Torarin saw that the dog had been waiting outside the parsonage his uneasiness came back. "What, Grim, why do you stay outside the gate all the evening? Why did you not go into the house and have your supper?" he said to the dog. "Can there be aught of ill awaiting Herr Arne? Maybe I have seen him for the last time. But even a strong man like him must one day die, and he is near ninety years old."

He guided his horse into a road which led past the farm of Branehog to Odsmalskil.

When he was come to Branehog he saw sledges standing in the yard and lights shining through the cracks of the closed shutters.

Then Torarin said to Grim: "These folks are still up. I will go in and ask if they have been shapening knives here tonight."

He drove into the farmyard, but when he opened the door of the house he saw that a feast was being held. Upon the benches by the wall sat old men drinking ale, and in the middle of the room the young people played and sang.

Torarin saw at once that no man here thought of making his weapon ready for a deed of blood. He slammed the door again and would have gone his way, but the host came after him. He asked Torarin to stay, since he had come, and led him into the room.

Torarin sat for a good while enjoying himself and chatting with the peasants. They were in high good humour, and Torarin was glad to be rid of all his gloomy thoughts.

But Torarin was not the only latecomer to the feast that evening. Long after him a man and a woman entered the door. They were poorly clad and lingered bashfully in the corner between door and fireplace.

The host at once came forward to his two guests. He took the hand of each and led them up the room. Then he said to the others: "Is it not truly said that the shorter the way the more the delay? These are our nearest neighbors. Branehog had no other tenants besides them and me."

"Say rather there are none but you," said the man. "You cannot call me a tenant. I am only a poor charcoal-burner whom you have allowed to settle on your land."

The man seated himself beside Torarin and they began to converse. The newcomer told Torarin how it was he came so late to the feast. It was because their cabin had been visited by three strangers whom they durst not leave, three journeymen tanners who had been with them all day. When they came in the morning they were worn out and ailing; they said they had lost their way in the forest and had wandered about for a whole week. But after they had eaten and slept they soon recovered their strength, and when evening came they had asked which was the greatest and richest house thereabout, for thither they would go and seek for work. The wife had answered that the parsonage, where Herr Arne dwelt, was the best place. Then at once they had taken long knives out of their packs and begun to sharpen them. They were at this a good while, with such ferocious looks that the charcoal-burner and his wife durst not leave their home. "I can still see them as they sat grinding their knives," said the man. "They looked terrible with their great beards that had not been cut or tended for many a day, and they were clad in rough coats of skin, which were tattered and befouled. I thought I had three werewolves in the house with me, and I was glad when at last they took themselves off."

When Torarin heard this he told the charcoal-burner what he himself had witnessed at the parsonage.

"So it was true enough that this night they whetted knives at Branehog," said Torarin, laughing. He had drunk deeply, because of the sorrow and heaviness that were upon him when he came, seeking to comfort himself as best he could. "Now I am of good cheer again," said he, "since I am well assured it was no evil omen the parson's lady heard, but only these tanners making ready their gear."

Long after midnight a couple of men came out of the house at Branehog to harness their horses and drive home.

When they had come into the yard they saw

a great fire flaring up against the sky in the north. They hastened back into the house and cried out: "Come out! Come out! Solberga parsonage is on fire!"

There were many folks at the feast, and those who had a horse leapt upon his back and made haste to the parsonage; but those who had to run with their own swift feet were there almost as soon.

When the people came to the parsonage nobody was to be seen, nor was there any sign of movement; all seemed to be asleep, though the flames rose high into the air.

Yet it was none of the houses that burned, but a great pile of wood and straw and faggots that had been stacked against the wall of the old dwelling. It had not been burning long. The flames had done no more than blacken the sound timber of the wall and melt the snow on the thatched roof. But now they had begun to take hold of the thatch.

Everyone saw at once that this was arson. They began to wonder whether Herr Arne and his wife were really asleep, or whether some evil had befallen them.

But before the rescuers entered the house they took long poles and pulled away the burning faggots from the wall and clambered up to the roof to tear off the thatch, which had begun to smoke and was ready to catch fire.

Then some of the men went to the door of the house to enter and call Herr Arne; but when the first man came to the threshold he turned aside and made way for him who came next.

The second man took a step forward, but as he was about to grasp the door-handle he turned away and made room for those who stood behind him.

It seemed a ghastly door to open, for a broad stream of blood trickled over the threshold and the handle was besmeared with blood.

Then the door opened in their faces and Herr Arne's curate came out. He staggered toward the men with a deep wound in his head, and he was drenched with blood. For an instant he stood upright and raised his hand to command silence. Whereupon he spoke with the death rattle in his voice:

"This night Herr Arne and all his household have been murdered by three men who climbed down through the smoke-hole in the roof and were clad in rough skins. They threw themselves upon us like wild beasts and slew us."

He could utter no more. He fell down at the men's feet and was dead.

They then entered the room and found all as the curate had said.

The great oaken chest in which Herr Arne kept his money was gone, and Herr Arne's horse had been taken from the stable and his sledge from the shed.

Sledge tracks led from the yard across the glebe meadows down to the sea, and twenty men hastened away to seize the murderers. But the women set themselves to laying out the dead and carried them from the bloody room out upon the pure snow.

Not all of Herr Arne's household could be found; there was one missing. It was the poor little maid whom Herr Arne had taken into his house. There was much wondering whether, perchance, she had been able to escape, or whether the robbers had taken her with them.

But when they made careful search through the room they found her hidden away between the great stove and the wall. She had kept herself concealed there throughout the struggle and had taken no hurt at all, but she was so sick with terror that she could neither speak nor answer a question.

The poor maid who had escaped the butchery had been taken by Torarin to Marstrand. He had conceived so great pity for her that he had offered her lodging in his cramped cabin and a share of the food which he and his mother ate.

"This is the only thing I can do for Herr Arne," thought Torarin, "in return for all the times he has bought my fish and allowed me to sit at his table."

27

"Poor and lowly as I am," thought Torarin, "it is better for the maid that she go with me to the town than that she stay here among the country folk. In Marstrand are many rich burgesses, and perhaps the young maid may take service with one of them and so be well cared for."

When first the girl came to the town she sat and wept from morning to night. She bewailed Herr Arne and his household, and lamented that she had lost all who were dear to her. Most of all she wept for her foster sister, and said she wished she had not hidden herself against the wall, so that she might have shared death with her.

Torarin's mother said nothing to this so long as her son was at home. But when he had gone on his travels again she said one morning to the girl:

"I am not rich enough, Elsalill, to give you food and clothing that you may sit with your hands in your lap and nurse your sorrow. Come with me down to the quays and learn to clean fish."

So Elsalill went with her down to the quays and stood all day working among the other fish cleaners.

But most of the women on the quays were young and merry. They began to talk to Elsalill and asked her why she was so silent and sorrowful.

Then Elsalill began to tell them of the terrible thing that had befallen her no more than three nights ago. She spoke of the three robbers who had broken into the house by the smoke-hole in the roof and murdered all who were near and dear to her.

As Elsalill told her tale a black shadow fell across the table at which she worked. And when she looked up three fine gentlemen stood before her, wearing broad hats with long feathers and velvet clothes with great puffs, embroidered in silk and gold.

One of them seemed to be of higher rank than the others; he was very pale, his chin was shaven, and his eyes sat deep in his head. He looked as though he had lately been ill. But in all else he seemed a gay and bold-faced cavalier, who walked on the sunny quays to show his fine clothes and his handsome face.

Elsalill broke off both work and story.

29

She stood looking at him with open mouth and staring eyes. And he smiled at her.

"We are not come hither to frighten you, mistress," said he, "but to beg that we too may listen to your tale."

Poor Elsalill! Never in her life had she seen such a man. She felt she could not speak in his presence; she merely held her peace and cast her eyes upon her work.

The stranger began again: "Be not afraid of us, mistress! We are Scotsmen who have been in the service of King John of Sweden ten full years, but now have taken our discharge and are bound for home. We have come to Marstrand to find a ship for Scotland, but when we came hither we found every channel and firth frozen over, and here we must bide and wait. We have no business to employ us, and therefore we range about the quays to meet whom we may. We should be happy, mistress, if you would let us hear your tale."

Elsalill knew that he had talked thus long to let her recover from her emotion. At last she thought to herself: "You can surely show that you are not too homely to speak to a noble gentleman, Elsalill! For you are a maiden of good birth and no fisher lass."

"I was but telling of the great butchery at Solberga parsonage," said Elsalill. "There are so many who have heard that story."

"Yes," said the stranger, "but I did not know till now that any of Herr Arne's household had escaped alive."

Then Elsalill told once more of the wild robbers' deed. She spoke of how the old serving-men had gathered about Herr Arne to protect him and how Herr Arne himself had snatched his sword from the wall and pressed upon the robbers, but they had overcome them all. And the old mistress had taken up her husband's sword and set upon the robbers, but they had only laughed at her and felled her to the floor with a billet of wood. And all the other women had crouched against the wall of the stove, but when the men were dead the robbers came and pulled them down and slew them. "The last they slew," said Elsalill, "was my dear foster sister. She begged for life so piteously, and two of them would have let her live; but the third said that all must die, and

31

he thrust his knife into her heart."

While Elsalill was speaking of murder and blood the three men stood still before her. They did not exchange a glance with each other, but their ears grew long with listening, and their eyes sparkled, and sometimes their lips parted so that the teeth glistened.

Elsalill's eyes were full of tears; not once did she look up whilst she was speaking. She did not see that the man before her had the eyes and teeth of a wolf. Only when she had finished speaking did she dry her eyes and look up at him.

But when he met Elsalill's glance his face changed in an instant. "Since you have seen the murderers so well, mistress," said he, "you would doubtless know them again if you met them?"

"I have no more than seen them by the light of the brands they snatched from the hearth to light their murdering," said Elsalill; "but with God's help I'll surely know them again. And I pray to God daily that I may meet them."

"What mean you by that, mistress?" asked the stranger. "Is it not true that the murderous vagabonds are dead?"

"Indeed, I have heard so," said Elsalill. "The peasants who set out after them followed their tracks from the parsonage down to a hole in the ice. Thus far they saw tracks of sledge-runners upon the smooth ice, tracks of a horse's hoofs, tracks of men with heavy nailed boots. But beyond the hole no tracks led on across the ice, and therefore the peasants supposed them all dead."

"And do you not believe them dead, Elsalill?" asked the stranger.

"Oh, yes, I think they must be drowned," said Elsalill; "and yet I pray to God daily that they may have escaped. I speak to God in this wise: 'Let it be so that they have only driven the horse and the sledge into the hole, but have themselves escaped.'"

"Why do you wish this, Elsalill?" asked the stranger.

The tender maid Elsalill, she flung back her head and her eyes shone like fire. "I would they were alive that I might find them out and seize them. I would they were alive that I might tear their hearts out. I would they were alive that I might see their bodies quartered and spiked upon the wheel."

"How do you think to bring all this about?" said the stranger. "For you are only a weak little maid."

"If they were living," said Elsalill, "I should surely bring their punishment upon them. Rather would I go to my death than let them go free. Strong and mighty they may be, I know it, but they would not be able to escape me."

At this the stranger smiled upon her, but Elsalill stamped her foot.

"If they were living, should I not remember that they have taken my home from me, so that I am now a poor lass, compelled to stand here on the cold quay and clean fish? Should I not remember that they have slain all those near to me, and should I not remember most of all the man who plucked my foster sister from the wall and slew her who was so dear to me?"

But when the tender little maid gave proof of such great wrath, the three Scottish campaigners burst out laughing. So full of merriment were they that they went off, lest

Elsalill might take offence. They walked across the harbour and up a narrow alley which led to the market-place. But long after they were out of sight Elsalill heard their roars of loud and scornful laughter.

A week after his death Herr Arne was buried in Solberga church, and on the same day an inquest was held upon the murder in the assize house at Branehog.

Now Herr Arne's fame was such throughout Bohuslen, and so many people came together on the day of his funeral, both from the mainland and the islands, that it was as though an army had assembled about its leader. And so great a concourse moved between Solberga church and Branehog that toward evening not an inch of snow could be seen that had not been trampled by men's feet.

But late in the evening, when all had gone their ways, came Torarin the fish hawker driving along the road from Branehog to Solberga.

Torarin had talked with many men in the course of the day; again and again had he told the story of Herr Arne's death. He had been well entertained too at the assize and had been made to empty many a mug of ale with travellers from afar.

Torarin felt dull and heavy and lay down upon his load. It saddened him to think that Herr Arne was gone, and as he approached the parsonage a yet more grievous thought began to torment him. "Grim, my dog," he said, "had I believed that warning of the knives I might have warded off the whole disaster. I often think of that, Grim, my dog. It disquiets my spirit, I feel as though I had had a part in taking Herr Arne's life. Now remember what I say—next time I hear such a thing I will hold it true and be guided by it!"

Now while Torarin lay dozing upon his load with eyes half closed, his horse went on as he pleased, and on coming to Solberga parsonage he turned into the yard from old habit and went up to the stable door, Torarin being all unwitting. Only with the stopping of the sledge did he rise up and look about him; and then he fell a-shuddering, when he saw that he was in the yard of a house where so many people had been murdered no more than a week before.

He seized the reins at once to turn his horse and drive into the road again, but at that moment he felt a hand upon his shoulder and looked round. Beside him stood old Olof the groom, who had served at the parsonage as long as Torarin could remember.

"Have you such haste to leave our house tonight, Torarin?" said the man. "Let be and come indoors! Herr Arne sits there waiting for you."

A thousand thoughts came into Torarin's head. He knew not whether he was dreaming or awake. Olof the groom, whom he saw standing alive and well beside him, he had seen a week before lying dead amongst the others with a great wound in his throat.

Torarin took a firmer hold of the reins. He thought the best thing for him was to make off as soon as he could. But Olof the groom's hand still lay upon his shoulder, and the old fellow gave him no peace.

Torarin racked his brains to find an excuse. "I had no thought of coming to disturb Herr Arne so late in the evening," said he. "My horse turned in here whilst I was unaware. I will go now and find a lodging for the night. If Herr Arne wishes to see me, I can well come again tomorrow."

With this Torarin bent forward and struck his horse with the slack of the reins to make him move off.

But at the same instant the parson's man was at the horse's head; he caught him by the bridle and forced him to stand still. "Cease your obstinacy, Torarin!" said the man. "Herr Arne is not yet gone to bed, he sits waiting for you. And you should know full well that you can have as good a night's lodging here as anywhere in the parish."

Torarin was about to answer that he could

not be served with lodging in a roofless house. But before speaking he raised his eyes to the dwelling house, and then he saw that the old timber hall stood unharmed and stately as before the fire. And yet that very morning Torarin had seen the naked rafters thrusting out into the air.

He looked and looked and rubbed his eyes, but there was no doubt of it, the parsonage stood there unharmed, with thatch and snow upon its roof. He saw smoke and sparks streaming up through the louver, and rays of light gleaming through the illclosed shutters upon the snow.

A man who travels far and wide on the cold highway knows no better sight than the gleam that steals out of a warm room. But the sight made Torarin even more terrified than before. He whipped up his horse till he reared and kicked, but not a step would he go from the stable door.

"Come in with me, Torarin!" said the groom. "I thought you had enough remorse already over this business."

Then Torarin remembered the promise he had made himself on the road and, though a moment before he had stood up and lashed his horse furiously, he was now meek as a lamb.

"Well, Olof groom, here am I!" he said, and sprang down from the sledge. "It is true that I wish to have no more remorse over this business. Take me in to Herr Arne!"

But it was with the heaviest steps he had ever known that Torarin went across the yard to the house.

When the door was opened Torarin closed his eyes to avoid looking into the room, but he tried to take heart by thinking of Herr Arne. "He has given you many a good meal. He has bought your fish, even when his own larder was full. He has always shown you kindness in his lifetime, and assuredly he will not harm you after death. Mayhap he has a service to ask of you. You must not forget, Torarin, that we are to show gratitude to the dead as to the living."

Torarin opened his eyes and looked down the room. He saw the great hall just as he had seen it before. He recognized the high brick stove and the woven tapestries that hung upon the walls. But he glanced many

times from wall to wall before daring to
raise his eyes to the table and the bench
where Herr Arne had been wont to sit.

At last he looked there, and then he saw
Herr Arne himself sitting in the flesh at the
head of the table with his wife on one side
and his curate on the other, as he had seen
him a week before. He seemed to have just
finished his meal, the dish was thrust away,
and his spoon lay on the table before him.
All the old men and women servants were
sitting at the table, but only one of the
young maids.

Torarin stood still a long time by the door
and watched them that sat at table. They
all looked anxious and mournful, and even
Herr Arne was gloomy as the rest and sup-
ported his head in his hand.

At last Torarin saw him raise his head.

"Have you brought a stranger into the
house with you, Olof groom?"

"Yes," answered the man, "it is Torarin
the fish hawker, who has been this day at
the assize at Branehog."

Herr Arne's looks seemed to grow more
cheerful at this, and Torarin heard him

45

say: "Come forward then, Torarin, and give us news of the assize! I have sat here and waited for half the night."

All this had such a real and natural air that Torarin began to feel more and more courageous. He walked quite boldly across the room to Herr Arne, asking himself whether the murder was not an evil dream and whether Herr Arne was not in truth alive.

But as Torarin crossed the room, his eyes from old habit sought the four-post bed, beside which the great money chest used to stand. But the ironbound chest was no longer in its place, and when Torarin saw that a shudder again passed through him.

"Now Torarin is to tell us how things went at the assize today," said Herr Arne.

Torarin tried to do as he was bid and tell of the assize and the inquest, but he could command neither his lips nor his tongue, and his speech was faulty and stammering, so that Herr Arne stopped him at once. "Tell me only the main thing, Torarin. Were our murderers found and punished?"

"No, Herr Arne," Torarin had the boldness to answer. "Your murderers lie at the bottom of Hakefjord. How would you have any take revenge on them?"

When Torarin returned this answer Herr Arne's old temper seemed to be kindled within him and he smote the table hard. "What is that you say, Torarin? Has the Governor of Bohus been here with judges and clerks and held assize and has no man had the wit to tell him where he may find my murderers?"

"No, Herr Arne," answered Torarin. "None among the living can tell him that."

Herr Arne sat awhile with a frown on his brow, staring dismally before him. Then he turned once more to Torarin.

"I know that you bear me affection, Torarin. Can you tell me how I may be revenged upon my murderers?"

"I can well understand, Herr Arne," said Torarin, "that you wish to be revenged upon those who so cruelly have deprived you of your life. But there is none amongst us who walk God's earth that can help you in this."

Herr Arne fell into a deep brooding when he heard this answer.

47

There was a long silence. After a while Torarin ventured to put forward a request. "I have now fulfilled your desire, Herr Arne, and told you how it went at the assize. Have you aught else to ask me, or will you now let me go?"

"You are not to go, Torarin," said Herr Arne, "until you have answered me once more whether none of the living can give us vengeance."

"Not if all the men in Bohuslen and Norway came together to be revenged upon your murderers would they be able to find them," said Torarin.

Then said Herr Arne: "If the living cannot help us, we must help ourselves."

With this Herr Arne began in a loud voice to say a paternoster, not in Norse but in Latin, as had been the use of the country before his time. And as he uttered each word of the prayer he pointed with his finger at one of those who sat with him at the table. He went through them all in this way many times, until he came to Amen. And as he spoke this word his finger pointed at the young maid who was his niece.

The young maid rose at once from the bench, and Herr Arne said to her: "You know what you have to do."

Then the young maiden lamented and said: "Do not send me upon this errand! It is too heavy a charge to lay upon so tender a maid as I."

"You shall assuredly go," said Herr Arne. "It is right that you go, since you have most to revenge. None of us has been robbed of so many years of life as you, who are the youngest among us."

"I desire not to be revenged on any man," said the maiden.

"You are to go at once," said Herr Arne. "And you will not be alone. You know that there are two among the living who sat with us here at table a week ago."

But when Torarin heard these words he thought they meant that Herr Arne charged him to contend with malefactors and murderers, and he cried out: "By the mercy of God I conjure you, Herr Arne——"

At that moment it seemed to Torarin that both Herr Arne and the parsonage vanished in a mist, and he himself sank down as though he had fallen from a giddy height, and with that he lost consciousness.

When he came to himself again dawn was breaking and he saw that he was lying on the ground in the yard of Solberga parsonage. His horse stood beside him with the sledge, and Grim barked and howled over him.

"It was all but a dream," said Torarin; "now I see that. The house is deserted and in ruin. I have seen neither Herr Arne nor any other. But I was so startled by the dream that I fell off the load."

4

When Herr Arne had
been dead a fortnight there came some nights
of clear, bright moonlight, and one evening
Torarin was out with his sledge. He checked
his horse time after time, as though he had
difficulty in finding the way. Yet he was not
driving through any trackless forest, but upon
what looked like a wide and open plain,
above which rose a number of rocky knolls.

The whole tract was covered with glit-
tering white snow. It had fallen in calm

weather and lay evenly, not in drifts and eddies. As far as the eye could see there was nothing but the same even plain and the same rocky knolls.

"Grim, my dog," said Torarin, "if we saw this tonight for the first time we should think we were driving over a great heath. But still we should wonder that the ground was so even and the road free from stones and ruts. What sort of tract can this be, we should say, where there are neither ditches nor fences, and how comes it that no grass or bushes stick up through the snow? And why do we see no rivers and streams, which elsewhere are wont to draw their black furrows through the white fields even in the hardest frost?"

Torarin was delighted with these fancies, and Grim too found pleasure in them. He did not move from his place on the load, but lay still and blinked.

But just as Torarin had finished speaking he drove past a lofty pole to which a broom was fastened.

"If we were strangers here, Grim, my dog," said Torarin, "we might well ask ourselves what sort of heath this was, where they set up such marks as we use at sea. 'This can never be the sea itself?' we should say at last. But we should think it utterly impossible. This that lies so firm and fast, can this be only water? And all the rocky knolls that we see so firmly united, can they be only holms and skerries parted by the rolling waves? No, we should never believe it was possible, Grim, my dog."

Torarin laughed and Grim still lay quiet and did not stir. Torarin drove on, until he rounded a high knoll. Then he gave a cry as though he had seen something strange. He put on an air of great surprise, dropped the reins and clapped his hands.

"Grim, my dog, so you would not believe this was the sea! Now you can tell what it is. Stand up, and then you will see that there is a big ship lying before us! You would not recognize the beacons, but this you cannot mistake. Now I think you will not deny that this is the sea itself we are driving over."

Torarin stayed still awhile longer as he gazed at a great vessel which lay frozen in.

She looked altogether out of place as she lay with the smooth and even snowfields all about her.

But when Torarin saw a thin column of smoke rising from the vessel's poop he drove up and hailed the skipper to hear if he would buy his fish. He had but a few codfish left at the bottom of his load, since in the course of the day he had been round to all the vessels which were frozen in among the islands, and sold off his stock.

On board were the skipper and his crew, and time was heavy on their hands. They bought fish of the hawker, not because they needed it, but to have someone to talk to.

When they came down on to the ice, Torarin put on an innocent air.

He began to speak of the weather. "In the memory of man there has not been such fine weather as this year," said Torarin. "For wellnigh three weeks we have had calm weather and hard frost. This is not what we are used to in the islands."

But the skipper, who lay there with his great gallias full-laden with herring barrels, and who had been caught by the ice in a bay near Marstrand just as he was ready to put to sea, gave Torarin a sharp look and said: "So then you call this fine weather?"

"What should I call it else?" said Torarin, looking as innocent as a child. "The sky is clear and calm and blue, and the night is fair as the day. Never before have I known the time when I could drive about the ice week after week. It is not often the sea freezes out here, and if once and again the ice has formed, there has always come a storm to break it up a few days after."

The skipper still looked black and glum; he made no answer to all Torarin's chat. Then Torarin began asking him why he never found his way to Marstrand. "It is no more than an hour's walk over the ice," said Torarin. But again he received no answer. Torarin could see that the man feared to leave his ship an instant, lest he might not be at hand when the ice broke up. "Seldom have I seen eyes so sick with longing," thought Torarin.

But the skipper, who had been held icebound among the skerries day after day, unable to hoist his sails and put to sea, had been busy the while with many thoughts, and he said to Torarin: "You are a man who travels much abroad and hears much news of all that happens: can you tell me why God has barred the way to the sea so long this year, keeping us all in captivity?"

As he said this Torarin ceased to smile, but put on an ignorant air and said: "I cannot see what you mean by that."

"Well," said the skipper, "I once lay in the harbour of Bergen a whole month, and a contrary wind blew all that time, so that no ship could come out. But on board one of the ships that lay there wind-bound was a man who had robbed churches, and he would have gone free but for the storm. Now they had time to search him out, and as soon as he had been taken ashore there came good weather and a fair wind. Now do you understand what I mean when I ask you to tell me why God keeps the gates of the sea barred?"

Torarin was silent awhile. He had a look as though he would make an earnest answer. But he turned it aside and said: "You have caught the melancholy with sitting here a prisoner among the skerries. Why do you not come in to Marstrand? I can tell you there is a merry life with hundreds of strangers in the town. They have naught else to do but drink and dance."

"How can it be they are so merry there?" asked the skipper.

"Oh," said Torarin, "there are all the seamen whose ships are frozen in like yours. There is a crowd of fishermen who had just finished their herring catch when the ice stayed them from sailing home. And there are a hundred Scottish mercenaries discharged from service, who lie here waiting for a ship to carry them home to Scotland. Do you think all these men would hang their heads and lose the chance of making merry?"

"Ay, it may well be that they can divert themselves, but, as for me, I have a mind to stay out here."

Torarin gave him a rapid glance. The skipper was a tall man and thin; his eyes were bright and clear as water, with a melancholy look in them. "To make that man merry is more than I or any other can do," thought Torarin.

Again the skipper began of his own accord to ask a question. "These Scotsmen," he said, "are they honest folk?"

"Is it you, maybe, that are to take them over to Scotland?" asked Torarin.

"Well," said the skipper, "I have a cargo for Edinburgh, and one of them was here but now and asked me would I take them. But I have small liking to sail with such wild companions aboard and I asked for time to think on it. Have you heard aught of them? Think you I may venture to take them?"

"I have heard no more of them but that they are brave men. I doubt not but you may safely take them."

But no sooner had Torarin said this than his dog rose from the sledge, threw his nose in the air, and began to howl.

Torarin broke off his praises of the Scotsmen at once. "What ails you now, Grim, my dog?" he said. "Do you think I stay here too long, wasting the time in talk?"

He made ready to drive off. "Well, God

be with you all!" he cried.

Torarin drove in to Marstrand by the narrow channel between Klovero and Koo. When he had come within sight of the town, he noticed that he was not alone on the ice.

In the bright moonlight he saw a tall man of proud bearing walking in the snow. He could see that he wore a plumed hat and rich clothes with ample puffs. "Hallo!" said Torarin to himself; "there goes Sir Archie, the leader of the Scots, who has been out this evening to bespeak a passage to Scotland."

Torarin was so near to the man that he drove into the long shadow that followed him. His horse's hoofs were just touching the shadow of the hat plumes.

"Grim," said Torarin, "shall we ask if he will drive with us to Marstrand?"

The dog began to bristle up at once, but Torarin laid his hand upon his back. "Be quiet, Grim, my dog! I can see that you have no love for the Scotsmen."

Sir Archie had not noticed that any one was so close to him. He walked on without

looking round. Torarin turned very quietly to one side in order to pass him.

But at that moment Torarin saw behind
the Scottish gallant something that looked
like another shadow. He saw something long
and thin and gray, which floated over the
white surface without leaving footprints in
the snow or making it crunch.

The Scotsman advanced with long and
rapid strides, looking neither to the right
hand nor to the left. But the gray shadow
glided on behind him, so near that it seemed
as though it would whisper something in
his ear.

Torarin drove slowly on till he came
abreast of them. Then he could see the
Scotsman's face in the bright moonlight.
He walked with a frown on his brow and
seemed vexed, as though full of thoughts
that displeased him.

Just as Torarin drove past, he turned
about and looked behind him as though
aware of someone following.

Torarin saw plainly that behind Sir Archie
stole a young maid in a long gray garment,
but Sir Archie did not see her. When he

turned his head she stood motionless, and Sir Archie's own shadow fell upon her, dark and broad, and hid her.

Sir Archie turned again at once and pursued his way, and again the maiden hurried forward and made as though she would whisper in his ear.

But when Torarin saw this his terror was more than he could bear. He cried aloud and whipped up his horse, so that it brought him at full gallop and dripping with sweat to the door of his cabin.

5

The town with all
its houses and buildings stood upon that
side of Marstrand island which looked to
landward and was protected by a wreath
of holms and islets. There people swarmed
in its streets and alleys; there lay the harbour, full of ships and boats, the quays,
with folk busy gutting and salting fish;
there lay the church and churchyard, the
market and town hall, and there stood many
a lofty tree and waved its green branches

in summer time.

But upon that half of Marstrand island which looked westward to the sea, unguarded by isles or skerries, there was nothing but bare and barren rocks and ragged headlands thrust out into the waves. Heather there was in brown tufts and prickly thorn bushes, holes of the otter and the fox, but never a path, never a house or any sign of man.

Torarin's cabin stood high up on the ridge of the island, so that it had the town on one side and the wilderness on the other. And when Elsalill opened her door she came out upon broad, naked slabs of rock, from which she had a wide view to the westward, even to the dark horizon of the open sea.

All the seamen and fishermen who lay icebound at Marstrand used to pass Torarin's cabin to climb the rocks and look for any sign of the ice parting in the coves and sounds.

Elsalill stood many a time at the cottage door and followed with her eyes the men who mounted the ridge. She was sick at heart from the great sorrow that had befallen her, and she said to herself: "I think everyone is happy who has something to look for. But I have nothing in the wide world on which to fix my hopes."

One evening Elsalill saw a tall man, who wore a broad-brimmed hat with a great feather, standing upon the rocks and gazing westward over the sea like all the others.

And Elsalill knew at once that the man was Sir Archie, the leader of the Scots, who had talked with her on the quay.

As he passed the cabin on his way home to the town, Elsalill was still standing in the doorway, and she was weeping.

"Why do you weep?" he asked, stopping before her.

"I weep because I have nothing to long for," said Elsalill. "When I saw you standing upon the rocks and looking out over the sea, I thought: 'He has surely a home beyond the water, and there he is going.' "

Then Sir Archie's heart was softened, and it made him say: "It is many a year since any spoke to me of my home. God knows how it fares with my father's house. I left it when I was seventeen to serve in the wars abroad."

On saying this Sir Archie entered the cottage with Elsalill and began to talk to her of his home.

And Elsalill sat and listened to Sir Archie, who spoke both long and well. Each word that came from his lips made her feel happy. But when the time drew on for Sir Archie to go, he asked if he might kiss her.

Then Elsalill said No, and would have slipped out of the door, but Sir Archie stood in her way and would have made her kiss him.

At that moment the door of the cottage opened, and its mistress came in in great haste.

Then Sir Archie drew back from Elsalill. He simply gave her his hand in farewell and hurried away.

But Torarin's mother said to Elsalill: "It was well that you sent for me, for it is not fitting for a maid to sit alone in the house with such a man as Sir Archie. You know full well that a soldier of fortune has neither honour nor conscience."

"Did I send for you?" asked Elsalill,

astonished.

"Yes," answered the old woman. "As I stood at work on the quay there came a little maid I had never seen before, and brought me word that you begged me to go home."

"How did this maid look?" asked Elsalill.

"I heeded her not so closely that I can tell you how she looked," said the old woman. "But one thing I marked; she went so lightly upon the snow that not a sound was heard."

When Elsalill heard this she turned very pale and said: "Then it must have been an angel from heaven who brought you the message and led you home."

Another time Sir Archie sat in Torarin's cabin and talked with Elsalill.

There was no one beside them; they talked gaily together and were very cheerful.

Sir Archie was telling Elsalill that she must go home with him to Scotland. There he would build her a castle and make her a fine lady. He told her she should have a hundred serving-maids to wait upon her, and she should dance at the court of the King.

Elsalill sat silently listening to every word Sir Archie said to her, and she believed them all. And Sir Archie thought that never had he met a damsel so easy to beguile as Elsalill.

Suddenly Sir Archie ceased speaking and looked down at his left hand.

"What is it, Sir Archie? Why do you say no more?" asked Elsalill.

Sir Archie opened and closed his hand convulsively. He turned it this way and that.

"What is it, Sir Archie?" asked Elsalill. "Does your hand pain you on a sudden?"

Then Sir Archie turned to Elsalill with a startled face and said: "Do you see this hair, Elsalill, that is wound about my hand? Do you see this lock of fair hair?

When he began to speak the girl saw nothing, but ere he had finished she saw a coil of fine, fair hair wind itself twice about Sir Archie's hand.

And Elsalill sprang up in terror and cried out: "Sir Archie, whose hair is it that is bound about your hand?"

Sir Archie looked at her in confusion, not knowing what to say. "It is real hair, Elsalill, I can feel it. It lies soft and cool about my hand. But whence did it come?"

The maid sat staring at his hand, and it seemed that her eyes would fall out of her head.

"So was it that my foster sister's hair was wound about the hand of him who murdered her," she said.

But now Sir Archie burst into a laugh. He quickly drew back his hand.

"Why," said he, "you and I, Elsalill, we are frightening ourselves like little children. It was nothing more than a bright sunbeam falling through the window."

But the girl fell to weeping and said: "Now methinks I am crouching again by the stove and I can see the murderers at their work. Ah, but I hoped to the last they would not find my dear foster sister, but then one of them came and plucked her from the wall, and when she sought to escape he twined her hair about his hand and held her fast. And she fell on her knees before him and said: 'Have pity on my youth! Spare my life, let me live long enough to know why I have come into the world! I have done you no ill, why would you kill me? Why would you deny me my life?' But he paid no heed to her words and killed her."

While Elsalill said this Sir Archie stood with a frown on his brow and turned his eyes away.

"Ah, if I might one day meet that man!" said Elsalill. She stood before Sir Archie with clenched fists.

"You cannot meet the man," said Sir Archie. "He is dead."

But the maid threw herself upon the bench and sobbed. "Sir Archie, Sir Archie, why have you brought the dead into my thoughts? Now I must weep all evening and all night. Leave me, Sir Archie, for now I have no thought for any but the dead. Now I can only think upon my foster sister and how dear she was to me."

And Sir Archie had no power to console her, but was banished by her tears and wailing and went back to his companions.

Sir Archie could not understand why his mind was always so full of heavy thoughts. He could never escape them, whether he drank with his companions, or whether he sat in talk with Elsalill. If he danced all night at the wharves they were still with him, and if he walked far and wide over the frozen sea, they followed him there.

"Why am I ever forced to remember what I would fain forget?" Sir Archie asked himself. "It is as though someone were always stealing behind me and whispering in my ear.

"It is as though someone were weaving a net about me," said Sir Archie, "to catch all my own thoughts and leave me none but this. I cannot see the pursuer who casts the net, but I can hear his step as he comes stealing after me."

"It is as though a painter went before me and painted the same picture wherever my eyes may rest," said Sir Archie. "Whether

I look to heaven or to earth I see naught else but this one thing."

"It is as though a mason sat within my heart and chiselled out the same heavy care," said Sir Archie. "I cannot see this mason, but day and night I can hear the blows of his mallet as he hammers at my heart. 'Heart of stone, heart of stone,' he says, 'now you shall yield. Now I shall hammer into you a lasting care.'"

Sir Archie had two friends, Sir Philip and Sir Reginald, who followed him wherever he went. They were grieved that he was always cast down and that nothing could avail to cheer him.

"What is it that ails you?" they would say. "What makes your eyes burn so, and why are your cheeks so pale?"

Sir Archie would not tell them what it was that tormented him. He thought: "What would my comrades say of me if they knew I yielded to these unmanly thoughts? They would no longer obey me if they found out that I was racked with remorse for a deed there was no avoiding."

As they continued to press him, he said

at last, to throw them off the scent: "Fortune is playing me strange tricks in these days. There is a girl I have a mind to win, but I cannot come at her. Something always stands in my way."

"Maybe the maiden does not love you?" said Sir Reginald.

"I surely think her heart is disposed toward me," said Sir Archie; "but there is something watching over her, so that I cannot win her."

Then Sir Reginald and Sir Philip began to laugh and said: "Never fear, we'll get you the girl."

That evening Elsalill was walking alone up the lane, coming from her work. She was tired and thought to herself: "This is a hard life and I find no joy in it. It sickens me to stand all day in the reek of fish. It sickens me to hear the other women laugh and jest in their rude voices. It sickens me to see the hungry gulls fly above the tables trying to snatch the fish out of my hands. Oh, that someone would come and take me away from here! I would follow him to the world's end."

When Elsalill had reached the darkest part of the lane, Sir Reginald and Sir Philip came out of the shadow and greeted her.

"Mistress Elsalill," they said, "we have a message for you from Sir Archie. He is lying sick at the inn. He longs to speak with you and begs you to accompany us home."

Elsalill began to fear that Sir Archie might be grievously sick, and she turned at once and went with the two Scottish gallants who were to bring her to him.

Sir Philip and Sir Reginald walked one on each side of her. They smiled at one another and thought that nothing could be easier than to delude Elsalill.

Elsalill was in great haste; she almost ran down the lane. Sir Philip and Sir Reginald had to take long strides to keep up with her.

But as Elsalill was making such haste to reach the inn, something began to roll before her feet. It seemed to have been thrown down in front of her, and she nearly stumbled over it.

"What can it be that rolls on and on

before my feet?" thought Elsalill. "It must be a stone that I have kicked from the ground and sent rolling down the hill."

She was in such a hurry to reach Sir Archie that she did not like being hindered by the thing that rolled close before her feet. She kicked it aside, but it came back at once and rolled before her down the lane.

Elsalill heard it ring like silver when she kicked it away, and she saw that it was bright and shining.

"It is no common stone," she thought. "I believe it is a coin of silver." But she was in such haste to reach Sir Archie that she thought she had no time to pick it up.

But again and again it rolled before her feet, and she thought: "You will go on the faster if you stoop down and pick it up. You can throw it far away if it is nothing."

She stooped down and picked it up. It was a big silver coin and it shone white in her hand.

"What is it that you have found in the street, mistress?" asked Sir Reginald. "It shines so white in the moonlight."

At that moment they were passing one of the great storehouses, where foreign fisher-folk lodged while they lay at Marstrand. Before the entrance hung a lantern, which threw a feeble light upon the street.

"Let us see what you have found, mistress," said Sir Philip, standing under the light.

Elsalill held up the coin to the lantern, and hardly had she cast eye upon it when she cried out: "This is Herr Arne's money! I know it well. This is Herr Arne's money!"

"What's that you say, mistress?" asked Sir Reginald. "What makes you say it is Herr Arne's money?"

"I know the coin," said Elsalill. "I have often seen it in Herr Arne's hand. Yes, it is surely Herr Arne's money."

"Shout not so loudly, mistress!" said Sir Philip. "People run here already to know the cause of this outcry."

But Elsalill paid no heed to Sir Philip. She saw that the door of the warehouse stood open. A fire blazed in the midst of the floor and round about it sat a number of men conversing quietly and at leisure.

Elsalill hastened in to them, holding the coin aloft. "Listen to me, every man!" she cried. "Now I know that Herr Arne's murderers are alive. Look here! I have found one of Herr Arne's coins."

All the men turned toward her. She saw that Torarin the fish hawker sat among them.

"What is that you tell us so noisily, my girl?" Torarin asked. "How can you know Herr Arne's moneys from any other?"

"Well may I know this very piece of silver from any other," said Elsalill. "It is old and heavy, and it is chipped at the edge. Herr Arne told us that it came from the time of the old kings of Norway, and never would he part with it when he counted out money to pay for his goods."

"Now you must tell us where you have found it, mistress," said another of the fishermen.

"I found it rolling before me in the street," said Elsalill. "One of the murderers has surely dropped it there."

"It may be as you say," said Torarin, "but what can we do in this matter? We cannot find the murderers by this alone, that you know they have walked in one of our streets."

The fishermen were agreed that Torarin had spoken wisely. They settled themselves again about the fire.

"Come home with me, Elsalill," said Torarin. "This is not an hour for a young maid to run about the streets of the town."

As Torarin said this, Elsalill looked about for her companions. But Sir Reginald and Sir Philip had stolen away without her noticing their departure.

6

One morning the hostess of the Town Cellars at Marstrand threw open her doors to sweep the steps and the lobby, and then she caught sight of a young maid sitting on one of the steps and waiting. She was dressed in a long gray garment which was fastened with a belt at the waist. Her hair was fair, and it was neither bound nor braided, but hung down on either side of her face.

As the door opened she went down the

steps into the lobby, but it seemed to the hostess that she moved as though walking in her sleep. And all the time she kept her eyelids lowered and her arms pressed close to her side. The nearer she came, the more astonished was the hostess at the fragile slenderness of her form. Her face was fair, but it was delicate and transparent, as though it had been made of brittle glass.

When she came down to the hostess she asked whether there was any work she could do, and offered her services.

Then the hostess thought of all the wild companions whose habit it was to sit drinking ale and wine in her tavern, and she could not help smiling. "No, there is no place here for a little maid like you," she said.

The maiden did not raise her eyes nor make the slightest movement, but she asked again to be taken into service. She desired neither board nor wages, she said, only to have a task to perform.

"No," said the hostess, "if my own daughter were as you are, I should refuse her this. I wish you a better lot than to be servant here."

The young maid went quietly up the steps, and the hostess stood watching her. She looked so small and helpless that the woman took pity on her.

She called her back and said to her: "Maybe you run greater risks if you wander alone about the streets and alleys than if you come to me. You may stay with me today and wash the cups and dishes, and then I shall see what you are fit for."

The hostess took her to a little closet she had contrived beyond the hall of the tavern. It was no bigger than a cupboard and had neither window nor loophole, but was only lighted by a hatch in the wall of the public room.

"Stand here today," said the hostess to the maid, "and wash me all the cups and dishes I pass you through this hatch, then I shall see whether I can keep you in my service."

The maiden went into the closet, and she moved so silently that the hostess thought it was like a dead woman slipping into her grave.

She stood the whole day and spoke to none, nor ever leaned her head through the hatch to look at the folk who came and went in the tavern. And she did not touch the food that was set before her.

Nobody heard her make a clatter as she washed, but whenever the hostess held out her hand to the hatch, she passed out clean cups and dishes without a speck on them.

But when the hostess took them to set them out on the table, they were so cold that she thought they would sear the skin off her fingers. And she shuddered and said: "It is as though I took them from the cold hands of Death himself."

One day there had been no fish to clean on the quays, so that Elsalill had stayed at home. She sat at the spinning-wheel and was alone in the cottage. A good fire was burning on the hearth, and it was light enough in the room.

In the midst of her work she felt a light

breath, as though a cold breeze had swept over her forehead. She looked up and saw her dead foster sister standing beside her.

Elsalill laid her hand on the wheel to stop it, and sat still, looking at her foster sister. At first she was afraid, but she thought to herself: "It is unworthy of me to be afraid of my foster sister. Whether she be dead or alive, I am still glad to see her."

"Dear sister," she said to the dead girl, "is there aught you would have me do?"

The other said to her in a voice that had neither strength nor tone: "My sister Elsalill, I am in service at the tavern, and the hostess has made me stand and wash cups and dishes all day. Now the evening is come and I am so tired that I can hold out no longer. I have come hither to ask if you will not give me your help."

When Elsalill heard this it was as though a veil was drawn over her mind. She could no longer think nor wonder nor feel any fear. She only knew joy at seeing her foster sister again, and she answered: "Yes, dear sister, I will come straight and help you."

Then the dead girl went to the door, and Elsalill followed her. But as they stood on the threshold her foster sister paused and said to Elsalill: "You must put on your cloak. There is a strong wind outside." And as she said this her voice sounded clearer and less muffled than before.

Elsalill then took her cloak from the wall and wrapped it around her. She thought to herself: "My foster sister loves me still. She wishes me no evil. I am only happy that I may go with her wherever she may take me."

And then she followed the dead girl through many streets, all the way from Torarin's cabin, which stood on a rocky slope, down to the level streets about the harbour and the market place.

The dead girl always walked two paces in front of Elsalill. A heavy gale was blowing that evening, howling through the streets, and Elsalill noticed that when a violent gust would have flung her against the wall, the dead girl placed herself between her and the wind and screened her as well as she could with her slender body.

When at last they came to the town hall the dead girl went down the cellar steps and beckoned Elsalill to follow her. But as they were going down the wind blew out the light in the lantern that hung in the lobby and they were in darkness. Then Elsalill did not know where to turn her steps and the dead girl had to put her hand on hers to lead her. But the dead girl's hand was so cold that Elsalill started and began to quake with fear. Then the dead girl drew her hand away and wound it in a corner of Elsalill's cloak before she led her on again. But Elsalill felt the icy chill through fur and lining.

Now the dead girl led Elsalill through a long corridor and opened a door for her. They came into a little dark closet where a feeble light fell through a hatch in the wall. Elsalill saw that they were in a room where the scullery wench stood and scoured cups and dishes for the hostess to set out on the tables for her customers. Elsalill could just see that a pail of water stood upon a stool, and in the hatch were many cups and goblets that wanted rinsing.

"Will you help me with this work tonight, Elsalill?" said the dead girl.

"Yes, dear sister," said Elsalill, "you know I will help you with whatsoever you wish."

Elsalill then took off her cloak, rolled up her sleeves and began the work.

"Will you be very quiet and silent in here, Elsalill, so that the hostess may not know that I have found help?"

"Yes, dear sister," said Elsalill; "you may be sure I will."

"Then farewell, Elsalill," said the dead girl. "I have only one more thing to ask of you. And it is that you be not too angry with me for this thing."

"Wherefore do you bid me farewell?" said Elsalill. "I will gladly come every evening and help you."

"No, there is no need for you to come after this evening," said the dead girl. "I have good hope that tonight you will give me such help that my mission will now be ended."

As they spoke thus Elsalill was already leaning over her work. All was still for a while, but then she felt a light breath on her forehead, as when the dead girl had come to her in Torarin's cabin. She looked up and saw that she was alone. Then she knew what it was that had felt like a faint breeze upon her face, and said to herself: "My dead foster sister has kissed my forehead before she parted from me."

Elsalill now turned to her work and finished it. She rinsed out all the bowls and tankards and dried them. Then she looked in the hatch whether any more had been set in there, and finding none she stood at the hatch and looked out into the tavern.

It was an hour of the day when there was usually little custom in the cellars. The hostess was absent from her bar and none of her tapsters was to be seen in the room. The place was empty, save for three men, who sat at the end of a long table. They were guests, but they seemed well at their ease, for one of them, who had emptied his tankard, went to the bar, filled it from one of the great tuns of ale and wine that stood there, and sat down again to drink.

Elsalill felt as though she had come here from a strange world. Her thoughts were with her dead foster sister, and she could not clearly take in what she saw. It was a long while before she was aware that the three men at the table were well known and dear to her. For they who sat there were none other than Sir Archie and his two friends Sir Reginald and Sir Philip.

For some days past Sir Archie had not visited Elsalill, and she was glad to see him. She was on the point of calling to him that she was there at hand; but then the thought came to her, how strange it was that he had ceased to visit her, and she kept silence. "Maybe his fancy has turned to another," thought Elsalill. "Maybe it is of her he is thinking."

For Sir Archie sat a little apart from the others. He was silent and gazed steadily before him, without touching his drink. He took no part in the talk, and when his friends addressed a word to him, he was seldom at the pains to make them an answer.

Elsalill could hear that the others were trying to put life into him. They asked him why he had left drinking, and even sought to persuade him that he should go and talk with Elsalill and so recover his good humour.

"You are to pay no heed to me," said Sir Archie. "There is another that fills my thoughts. Still do I see her before me, and still do I hear the sound of her voice in my ears."

And then Elsalill saw that Sir Archie was gazing at one of the massive pillars that upheld the cellar roof. She saw, too, what till then she had not marked, that her foster sister stood beside that pillar and looked upon Sir Archie. She stood there quite motionless in her gray habit, and it was not easy to discover her, as she stood so close against the pillar.

Elsalill stood quite still looking into the room. She noted that her foster sister kept her eyes raised when she looked upon Sir Archie. During the whole time she was with Elsalill she had walked with her eyes upon the ground.

Now her eyes were the only thing about her that was ghastly. Elsalill saw that they were dim and filmed. They had no glance, and the light was not mirrored in them any more.

After a while Sir Archie began again to lament. "I see her every hour. She follows me wherever I go," he said.

He sat with his face toward the pillar where the dead girl stood, and stared at her. But Elsalill was sure that he did not see her. It was not of her he spoke, but of one who was ever in his thoughts.

Elsalill never left the hatch and followed with her eyes all that took place, thinking that most of all she wished to find out who it was that filled Sir Archie's thoughts.

Suddenly she was aware that the dead girl had taken her place on the bench beside Sir Archie and was whispering in his ear.

But still Sir Archie knew nothing of her being so close to him or of her whispering in his ear. He was only aware of her presence in the mortal dread that came over him.

Elsalill saw that when the dead girl had

sat for a few moments whispering to Sir Archie, he hid his face in his hands and wept. "Alas, would I had never found the maid!" he said. "I regret nothing else but that I did not let the maiden go when she begged me."

The other two Scotsmen ceased drinking and looked in alarm at Sir Archie, who thus laid aside all his manliness and yielded to remorse. For a moment they were perplexed, but then one of them went up to the bar, took the tallest tankard that stood there and filled it with red wine. He brought it to Sir Archie, clapped him on the shoulder and said: "Drink, brother! Herr Arne's hoard is not yet done. So long as we have coin to buy such wine as this, no cares need sit upon us."

But in the same instant as these words were spoken: "Drink, brother! Herr Arne's hoard is not yet done," Elsalill saw the dead girl rise from the bench and vanish.

And in that moment Elsalill saw before her eyes three men with great beards and rough coats of skin, struggling with Herr Arne's servants. And now it was plain to her that they were the three who sat in the cellar—Sir Archie, Sir Philip, and Sir Reginald.

Elsalill came out of the closet where she had stood and rinsed the hostess's cups, and softly closed the door behind her. In the narrow corridor outside she stopped and stood motionless leaning against the wall for nearly an hour.

As she stood there she thought to herself: "I cannot betray him. Let him be guilty of what evil he may, I love him with all my heart. I cannot send him to be broken upon the wheel. I cannot see them burn away his hands and feet."

The storm that had raged all day became more and more violent as evening wore on, and Elsalill could hear its roar as she stood in the darkness.

"Now the first storms of spring have come," she thought. "Now they have come in all their might to set the waters free and break up the ice. In a few days we shall have open sea, and then Sir Archie will sail from hence, never to return. No more misdeeds can he commit in this land. What profits it then if he be taken and suffer for his crime? Neither the dead nor the living have any comfort of it."

Elsalill drew her cloak about her. She thought she would go home and sit quietly at her work without betraying her secret to any one.

But before she had raised a foot to go, she changed her purpose and stayed.

She stood still listening to the roaring of the gale. Again she thought of the coming of spring. The snow would disappear and the earth put on its garment of green.

"Merciful heaven, what a spring will this be for me!" thought Elsalill. "No joy and no happiness can bloom for me after the chills of this winter.

"No more than a year ago I was so happy when winter was past and spring came," she thought. "I remember one evening which was so fair that I could not sit within doors. So I took my foster sister by the hand, and we went out into the fields to fetch green boughs and deck the stove."

She recalled to mind how she and her foster sister had walked along a green pathway. And there by the side of the way they had seen a young birch that had been cut down. The wood showed that it had been cut many days before. But now they saw that the poor lopped tree had begun to put forth leaves and its buds were bursting.

Then her foster sister had stopped and bent over the tree. "Ah, poor tree," she said, "what evil can you have done, that you are not suffered to die, though you are cut down? What makes you put forth leaves, as though you still lived?"

And Elsalill had laughed at her and answered: "Maybe it grows so sweet and green that he who cut it down may see the harm he has wrought and feel remorse."

But her foster sister did not laugh with her, and there were tears in her eyes.

"It is a great sin to fell a tree in leafing time, when it is so full of force that it cannot die. It is terrible for a dead man if he cannot rest in his grave. They who are dead have small comfort to look for;

neither love nor happiness can reach them. All the good they yet desire is that they may be left to sleep in peace. Well may I weep when you say this birch cannot die for thinking of its murderer. The hardest fate for one deprived of life is that he may not sleep in peace but must pursue his murderer. The dead have naught to long for but to be left to sleep in peace."

When Elsalill recalled these words she began to weep and wring her hands.

"My foster sister will not find rest in her grave," she said, "unless I betray my beloved. If I do not aid her in this, she must roam above ground without respite or repose. My poor foster sister, she has nothing more to hope for but to find peace in her grave, and that I cannot give her unless I send the man I love to be broken on the wheel."

Sir Archie came out of the tavern and went through the long corridor. The lantern hanging from the roof had now been lighted again, and by its light he saw that a young maid stood leaning against the wall.

She was so pale and stood so still that Sir Archie was afraid and thought: "There at last before my eyes stands the dead girl who haunts me every day."

As Sir Archie went past Elsalill he laid his hand on hers to feel if it was really a dead girl standing there. And her hand was so cold that he could not say whether it belonged to the living or the dead.

But as Sir Archie touched Elsalill's hand she drew it back, and then Sir Archie knew her again.

He thought she had come there for his sake, and great was his joy to see her. At once a thought came to him: "Now I know what I will do, that the dead girl may be appeased and cease to haunt me."

He took Elsalill's hands within his own and raised them to his lips. "God bless you for coming to me this evening, Elsalill!" he said.

But Elsalill's heart was sore afflicted. She

could not speak for tears, even so much as to tell Sir Archie she had not come there to meet him.

Sir Archie stood silent a long while, but he held Elsalill's hands in his the whole time. And the longer he stood thus, the clearer and more handsome did his face become.

"Elsalill," said Sir Archie, and he spoke very earnestly, "for many days I have not been able to see you, because I have been tormented by heavy thoughts. They have left me no peace, and I believed I should soon go out of my mind. But tonight it goes better with me and I no longer see before me the image that tormented me. And when I found you here, my heart told me what I had to do to be rid of my torment for all time."

He bent down to look into Elsalill's eyes, but as she stood with drooping eyelids he went on: "You are angry with me, Elsalill, because I have not been to see you for many days. But I could not come, for when I saw you I was reminded even more of what tortured me. When I saw you I was forced to think even more of a young maid to whom I have done wrong. Many others have I wronged in my lifetime, Elsalill, but my conscience plagues me for naught else but what I did to this young maid."

As Elsalill still said nothing, he took her hands again and raised them to his lips and kissed them.

"Now, listen, Elsalill, to what my heart said to me when I saw you standing here and waiting for me. 'You have done injury to one maiden,' it said, 'and for what you have made her suffer, you must atone to another. You shall take her to wife, and you shall be so good to her that she shall never know sorrow. Such faithfulness shall you show her that your love will be greater on the day of your death than on your wedding day.' "

Elsalill stood still as before with downcast eyes. Then Sir Archie laid his hand on her head and raised it. "You must tell me, Elsalill, whether you hear what I say," he said.

Then he saw that Elsalill was weeping so violently that great tears ran down her cheeks.

"Why do you weep, Elsalill?" asked Sir Archie.

"I weep, Sir Archie," said Elsalill, "because I have too great love for you in my heart."

Then Sir Archie came yet closer to Elsalill and put his arm around her. "Do you hear how the wind howls without?" said he. "That means that soon the ice will break up, and that ships again will be free to sail over to my native land. Tell me now, Elsalill, will you come with me, so that I may make good to you the evil I have done to another?"

Sir Archie continued to whisper to Elsalill of the glorious life that awaited her, and Elsalill began to think to herself: "Alas, if only I did not know what evil he had done! Then I would go with him and live happily."

Sir Archie came closer and closer to her, and when Elsalill looked up she saw that his face was bending over her and that he was about to kiss her on the forehead. Then she remembered the dead girl who had so lately been with her and kissed her. She tore herself free from Sir Archie and said: "No, Sir Archie, I will never go with you."

"Yes," said Sir Archie, "you must come with me, Elsalill, or else I shall be drawn down to my destruction."

He began to whisper to the girl ever more tenderly, and again she thought to herself: "Were it not more pleasing to God and men that he be allowed to atone for his evil life and become a righteous man? Whom can it profit if he be punished with death?"

As these thoughts were in Elsalill's mind two men came by on their way to the tavern. When Sir Archie marked that they cast curious eyes on him and the maid, he said to her: "Come, Elsalill, I will take you home. I would not that any should see you had come to the tavern for me."

Then Elsalill looked up, as though suddenly calling to mind that she had another duty to perform than that of listening to Sir Archie. But her heart smote her when she thought of betraying his crime. "If you deliver him to the hangman, I must break," her heart said to her. And Sir Archie drew the girl's cloak more tightly about her and led her out into the street. He walked with her all the way to Torarin's cabin, and she noticed that whenever the storm blew fiercely in their faces, he placed himself before her and screened her.

Elsalill thought, all the time they were walking: "My dead foster sister knew nothing of this, that he would atone for his crime and become a good man."

Sir Archie still whispered the tenderest words in Elsalill's ear. And the longer she listened to him, the more firmly she believed in him.

"It must have been that I might hear Sir Archie whisper such words as these in my ear that my foster sister called me forth," she thought. "She loves me so dearly. She desires not my unhappiness but my happiness."

And as they stopped before the cabin, Sir Archie asked Elsalill once more whether she would go with him across the sea. And Elsalill answered that with God's help she would go.

Next day the storm had ceased. The weather was now milder, but it had caused little shrinking of the ice and the sea was closed as fast as ever.

When Elsalill awoke in the morning she thought: "It is surely better that a wicked man repent and live according to God's commandments than that he be punished with death."

That day Sir Archie sent a messenger to Elsalill, and he brought her a heavy armlet of gold.

And Elsalill was glad that Sir Archie had thought of giving her pleasure, and she thanked the messenger and accepted the gift.

But when he was gone she fell to thinking that this armlet had been bought for her with Herr Arne's money. When she thought of this she could not endure to look on it. She plucked it from her arm and threw it far away.

"What will my life be, if I must always call to mind that I am living on Herr Arne's money?" she thought. "If I put a mouthful of food to my lips, must I not think of the stolen money? And if I have a new gown, will it not ring in my ears that it is bought with ill-gotten gold? Now at last I see that it is impossible for me to go with Sir Archie and join my life to his. I shall tell him this when he comes."

When evening was drawing on, Sir Archie came to her. He was in cheerful mood, he had not been plagued with evil thoughts, and he believed it was owing to his promise to make good to one maiden the wrong he had done another.

When Elsalill saw him and heard him speak she could not bring herself to tell him that she was sad at heart and would part from him.

All the sorrows which gnawed at her were forgotten as she sat listening to Sir Archie.

The next day was a Sunday, and Elsalill went to church. She was there both in the morning and in the evening.

As she sat during the morning service listening to the sermon, she heard someone weeping and sobbing close by.

She thought it was one of those who sat beside her in the pew, but whether she looked to right or left she saw none but calm and devout worshippers.

Nevertheless, she plainly heard a sound of weeping, and it seemed so near to her that she might have touched the one who wept by putting out her hand.

Elsalill sat listening to the sighing and sobbing, and thought to herself that she had never heard so sorrowful a sound.

"Who is it that is afflicted with such deep grief that she must shed these bitter tears?" thought Elsalill.

She looked behind her, and she leaned forward over the next pew to see. But all were sitting in silence, and no face was wet with tears.

Then Elsalill thought there was no need to ask or wonder, for indeed she had known from the first who it was that wept beside her. "Dear sister," she whispered, "why do you not show yourself to me, as you did but lately? For you must know that I would gladly do all I may to dry your tears."

She listened for an answer, but none came. All she heard was the sobbing of the dead girl beside her.

Elsalill tried to hearken to what the preacher was saying in the pulpit, but she could follow little of it. And she grew impatient and whispered: "I know one who has more cause to weep than any, and that is myself. Had not my foster sister revealed her murderer to me I might have sat here with a heart full of joy."

114

As she listened to the weeping she became more and more resentful, so that she thought: "How can my dead foster sister require of me that I shall betray the man I love? Never would she herself have done such a thing, if she had lived."

She was shut up in the pew, but she could scarcely sit still. She rocked backward and forward and wrung her hands. "Now this will follow me all day," she thought. "Who knows," she went on, growing more and more anxious, "who knows whether it will not follow me through life?"

But the sobbing beside her grew ever deeper and sadder, and at last her heart was touched in spite of herself, and she too began to weep. "She who weeps so must have a terribly heavy grief," she thought. "She must have to bear suffering heavier than any of the living can conceive."

When the service was over and Elsalill had come out of church, she heard the sobbing no longer. But all the way home she wept to herself because her foster sister could find no peace in her grave.

When the time of evensong came Elsalill

115

went again to the church, being constrained to know whether her foster sister still sat there weeping.

And as soon as Elsalill entered the church she heard her, and her soul trembled within her when she caught the sound of the sobbing. She felt her strength forsaking her and she had but one desire—to help the dead girl who was wandering among the living and knew no rest.

When Elsalill came out of church it was still light enough for her to see that one of those who walked before her left bloody footprints in the snow.

"Who can it be so poor that he goes barefoot and leaves bloody footprints in the snow?" she thought.

All those who walked before her seemed to be well-to-do folk. They were neatly dressed and well shod.

But the red footprints were not old. Elsalill could see they were made by one of the group that walked before her. "It is someone who is footsore from a long journey," she thought. "God grant he may not have far to go ere he find shelter and rest."

She had a strong desire to know who it was that had made this weary pilgrimage, and she followed the footprints, though they led her away from her home.

But suddenly she saw that all the church-goers had gone another way and that she was alone in the street. Nevertheless, the blood-red footprints were there as plain as before. "It is my poor foster sister who is going before me," she thought; and she owned to herself that she had guessed it all the time.

"Alas, my poor foster sister, I thought you went so lightly upon earth that your feet did not touch the ground. But none among the living can know how painful your pilgrimage must be."

The tears started to her eyes, and she sighed: "Could she but find peace in her grave! Woe is me that she must wander here so long, till she has worn her feet to bleeding!"

"Stay, my dear foster sister!" she cried. "Stay, that I may speak to you!"

But as she cried thus, she saw that the

footprints fell yet faster in the snow, as though the dead girl were hastening her steps.

"Now she flies from me. She looks no more for help from me," said Elsalill.

The bloody footprints made her quite frantic, and she cried out: "My dear foster sister, I will do all you ask if only you may find rest in your grave!"

So soon as Elsalill had uttered these words a tall, big woman who had followed her came up and laid a hand on her arm.

"Who may you be, crying and wringing your hands here in the street?" the woman asked. "You call to my mind a little maid who came to me on Friday looking for a place and then ran away from me. Or perhaps you are the same?"

"No, I am not the same," said Elsalill, but if, as I think, you are the hostess of the Town Cellars, then I know what maid it is you speak of."

"Then you can tell me why she took herself off and has not come back," said the hostess.

"She left you," said Elsalill, "because she

did not choose to hear the talk of all the evildoers who gather in your tavern."

"Many a wild companion comes to my tavern," said the hostess, "but among them are no evildoers."

"Yet the maid heard three that sat there talking among themselves," said Elsalill, "and one of them said: 'Drink, brother! Herr Arne's hoard is not yet done.'"

When Elsalill had said these words she thought: "Now I have helped my foster sister and told what I heard. Now may God help me that this woman pay no heed to my words; so I shall be quit."

But when she saw in the hostess's face that she believed her, she was afraid and would have run away.

But before she had time to move, the hostess's heavy hand had taken firm hold of her so that she could not escape.

"If you can witness that such words have been uttered in my tavern, mistress," said the hostess, "then you were best not to run away. For you must go with me to those who have the power to seize the murderers and bring them to justice."

8

E lsalill came into the
tavern wrapt in her long cloak and went
straight to a table where Sir Archie sat
drinking with his friends. A crowd of customers sat about the tables in the cellar,
but Elsalill took no heed of all the wondering glances that followed her, as she
went and sat down beside the man she
loved. Her only thought was to be with
Sir Archie in the few moments of freedom
which were left to him.

When Sir Archie saw Elsalill come and sit by him, he rose and moved with her to a table that stood far down the room, hidden by a pillar. She could see that he was displeased at her coming to meet him in a place where it was not the custom for young maids to show themselves.

"I have no long message to bring you, Sir Archie," said Elsalill; "but I would have you know that I cannot go with you to your own country."

When Sir Archie heard Elsalill speak thus he was in despair, since he feared that, if he lost Elsalill, the evil thoughts would again take possession of him.

"Why will you not go with me, Elsalill?" he asked.

Elsalill was as pale as death. Her thoughts were so confused that she scarce knew what answer she made him.

"It is a perilous thing to follow a soldier of fortune," she said. "For none can tell whether such a man will keep his plighted troth."

Before Sir Archie had time to answer, a sailor came into the tavern.

He went up to Sir Archie and told him he was sent by the skipper of the great gallias which lay in the ice behind Klovero. The skipper prayed Sir Archie and all his men to make ready their goods and come aboard that evening. The storm had sprung up again and the sea was clearing far away to the westward. It might well be that before daybreak they would have open water and could sail for Scotland.

"You hear what this man says?" said Sir Archie to Elsalill. "Will you come with me?"

"No," said Elsalill, "I will not go with you."

But in her heart she was very glad, for she thought: "Now belike it will turn out so that he may escape ere the watch can come and seize him."

Sir Archie rose and went over to Sir Philip and Sir Reginald and spoke to them of the message. "Get you back to the inn before me," he said, "and make all ready. I have a word or two yet to say to Elsalill."

When Elsalill saw that Sir Archie was

coming back to her, she waved her hands as though to prevent him. "Why do you come back, Sir Archie?" she said. "Why do you not hasten down to the sea as fast as your feet may carry you?"

For such was her love for Sir Archie. She had indeed betrayed him for her dear foster sister's sake, but her most fervent wish was that he might escape.

"No, first will I beg you once more to come with me," said Sir Archie.

"But you know, Sir Archie, that I cannot come with you," said Elsalill.

"Why can you not?" said Sir Archie. "You are a poor orphan, so forlorn and friendless that none will care what becomes of you. But if you come with me, I will make you a noble lady. I am a powerful man in my own country. You shall be clad in silk and gold, and you shall tread a measure at the King's court.

Elsalill was shaking with alarm at his delaying while flight was still open to him. She could scarce calm herself to answer: "Go hence, Sir Archie! You must tarry no longer to importune me."

"There is something I would say to you, Elsalill," said Sir Archie, and his voice became more tender as he spoke. "When first I saw you, my only thought was of tempting and beguiling you. In the beginning I promised you riches in jest, but since two nights ago I have meant honestly by you. And now it is my purpose and desire to make you my wife. You may trust in me, as I am a gentleman and a soldier."

At that moment Elsalill heard the march of armed men in the square outside. "If I go with him now," she thought, "he may yet escape. If I refuse, I drive him to destruction. It is for my sake he tarries here so long that the watch will lay hands on him. But how can I go with the man who has murdered all my dear ones?"

"Sir Archie," said Elsalill, and she hoped her words might startle him, "Do you not hear the tramp of armed men in the square?"

"Oh, yes, I hear it," said Sir Archie; "there has been some alehouse brawl, I doubt not. Let it not fright you, Elsalill; it is but some fishermen that have come to clapper-claws over their cups."

"Sir Archie," said Elsalill, "do you not hear them stand before the town hall?"

Elsalill was trembling from head to foot, but Sir Archie took no note of it; he was quite calm.

"Where else would you have them stand?" said Sir Archie. "They must bring the brawlers here to lay them by the heels in the watch house. Listen not to them, Elsalill, but to me, who ask you to follow me over the sea!"

But Elsalill tried once more to put fear into Sir Archie. "Sir Archie," she said, do you not hear the watch coming down the steps to the cellar?"

"Oh, yes, I hear them," said Sir Archie; "they will come here to empty a pot of ale, since their prisoners are safe under lock and key. Think not of them, Elsalill, but think how tomorrow you and I will be sailing the wide sea to my dear native land!"

But Elsalill was pale as a corpse, and she shook so that she could scarce speak. "Sir Archie," she said, "do you not see them speaking with the hostess yonder at the bar? They are asking her whether any of those they seek is within."

"I'll wager they are charging her to brew them a warm, strong drink this stormy night," said Sir Archie. "You need not quake and tremble so mightily, Elsalill. You can follow me without fear. I tell you that if my father would have me wed the noblest damsel in our land, I should now say her nay. Come with me over the sea in full security, Elsalill! Nothing awaits you there but joy and happiness."

More and more of the pikemen had collected about the door, and Elsalill was now beside herself with terror. "I cannot look on while they come and seize him," she thought. She leaned toward Sir Archie and whispered to him: "Do you not hear, Sir Archie? They are asking the hostess whether any of Herr Arne's murderers is here within."

Then Sir Archie threw a glance across the room and looked at the pikemen who were speaking with the hostess. But he did not rise and fly as Elsalill had expected:

he bent down and looked deeply into her eyes. "Is it you, Elsalill, who have discovered and betrayed me?" he asked.

"I have done it for my dear foster sister's sake, that she might have peace in her grave," said Elsalill. "God knows what it has cost me to do it. But now fly, Sir Archie! There is yet time. They have not yet barred all doors and lobbies."

"You wolf's cub!" said Sir Archie. "When first I saw you on the quay I thought I ought to kill you."

But Elsalill laid her hand on his arm. "Fly, Sir Archie! I cannot sit still and see them come and take you. If you will not fly without me, then in God's name I will go with you. But do not stay longer here for my sake, Sir Archie! I will do all you ask of me, if only you will save your life."

But now Sir Archie was very angry, and he spoke scornfully to Elsalill. "Now, mistress, you shall never go in gold-embroidered shoes through lofty castle halls. Now you may stay in Marstrand all your days and gut herrings. Never shall you wed a man who has castle and lands, Elsalill. Your man shall be a poor fisherman and your dwelling a cabin on a cold rock."

"Do you not hear them setting guards before all the doors to bar the way with their pikes?" asked Elsalill. "Why do you not hasten hence? Why do you not fly out upon the ice and hide yourself in a ship?"

"I do not fly because I have a mind to sit and talk with Elsalill," said Sir Archie. "Are you thinking that now there is an end of all your joy, Elsalill? Are you thinking that now there is an end of my hope of atoning for my crime?"

"Sir Archie," whispered Elsalill, rising from her seat in her terror; "now the men are all posted. Now they will catch and seize you. Make haste and fly! I shall come out to your ship, Sir Archie, if only you will fly."

"You need not be so frightened, Elsalill," said Sir Archie. "We have some time left to talk together. These fellows have no stomach to set upon me here, where I can defend myself. They mean to take me in the narrow stair. They think to spit me on their long pikes. And that is what you have always wished me, Elsa-lill."

But the more her terror gained on Elsalill, the calmer became Sir Archie. She never ceased praying him to fly, but he laughed at her.

"You need not be so sure, mistress, that these fellows can take me. I have come through greater dangers than this. I'll warrant I was harder put to it some months since in Sweden. Some slanderers had told King John that his Scots guard was disloyal to him. And the King believed them. He threw the three commanders into dungeon and sent their men out of his realm, and had them guarded till they had passed the border."

"Fly, Sir Archie, fly!" begged Elsalill.

"You need not be troubled for me, Elsalill," said Sir Archie with a hard laugh. "This evening I am myself again, my old humour is come back. I see no more the young maid that haunted me, and I shall hold my own, never fear. I will tell you

of those three who lay in King John's
dungeon. They stole out of the tower one
night, when their guards were drowsy with
liquor, and ran their ways. And then they
fled to the border. But so long as they
were in the Swedish king's land they durst
not betray themselves. They had no choice,
Elsalill, but to make themselves rough coats
of skin and give out that they were journeymen tanners travelling the country in search
of work."

Now Elsalill began to mark how changed
Sir Archie was toward her. And she knew
he hated her, since he had found out that
she had betrayed him.

"Speak not so, Sir Archie!" said Elsalill.

"Why should you play me false, just
when I trusted you most?" said Sir Archie.
"Now I am again the man I was. Now
none shall find me merciful. And now you'll
see, Fortune will favour me, as she has
done hitherto. Were we not in bad case,
I and my comrades, when at last we had
walked through all Sweden and come down
to the coast here? We had no money to buy
us honourable clothes. We had no money

to pay for our shipping to Scotland. We
knew no remedy but to break into Solberga parsonage."

"Speak no more of that!" said Elsalill.

"Yes, now you must hear all, Elsalill,"
said Sir Archie. "There is one thing you
know not, and it is that when first we
came into the house we went to Herr
Arne, roused him, and told him he must
give us money. If he gave it freely, we
would not harm him. But Herr Arne re-
sisted us with force, and so we had to
strike him down. And when we had dis-
patched him, we had to make an end of
all his household."

Elsalill interrupted Sir Archie no more,
but her heart felt cold and empty. She
shuddered as she looked upon Sir Archie,
for as he spoke a cruel and bloodthirsty
look came over him. "What was I about
to do?" she thought. "Have I been mad
and loved the man who murdered all my
dear ones? God forgive my sin!"

"When we thought all were dead," said
Sir Archie, "we dragged the heavy money
chest out of the house. Then we set fire

about it, that men might think Herr Arne had been burnt alive."

"I have loved a wolf of the woods," said Elsalill to herself. "And him I have tried to save from justice!"

"But we drove down to the ice and fled to sea," Sir Archie went on. "We had no fear so long as we saw the flames mounting to the sky, but when we saw them die down we took alarm. We knew then that neighbours had come and put out the fire, and that we should be pursued. So we drove back toward land, for we had seen the outlet of a stream where the ice was thin. We lifted the chest from the sledge and drove forward till the ice broke under the horse's hoofs. Then we let it drown and sprang off to one side. If you were aught but a little maid, Elsalill, you would see that this was bravely done. We acquitted ourselves like men."

Elsalill kept still; she felt a sharp pain tearing at her heart. But Sir Archie hated her and delighted to torment her. "Then we took our belts and fastened them to the chest and began to draw it. But as the chest left tracks in the ice, we went ashore and gathered twigs of spruce and laid them under the chest. Then we took off our boots and went over the ice without leaving a trace behind us."

Sir Archie paused to throw a scornful glance at Elsalill.

"Although we had prospered in all this, we were yet in bad case. Wherever we went our bloodstained clothes would betray us and we should be seized. But now listen, Elsalill, so that you may tell all those who would be at the pains to give us chase, that they may understand we are not of a sort to be lightly taken! Listen to this: As we came over the ice toward Marstrand here, we met our comrades and countrymen, who had been banished by King John from his land. They had not been able to leave Marstrand because of the ice, and they helped us in our need, so that we got clothes. Since then we have gone about here in Marstrand and been in no danger. And no danger would threaten us now, if you had not been faithless and played me false."

Elsalill sat still. This was too great a grief for her. She could scarce feel her heart beating.

But Sir Archie sprang up and cried: "And no ill shall befall us tonight either. Of that you shall be witness, Elsalill!"

In an instant he seized Elsalill in both his arms and raised her off her feet. And with Elsalill before him as a shield Sir Archie ran through the tavern to the doorway. And the men who were posted to guard the door levelled their long pikes at him, but they durst not use them for fear of hurting Elsalill.

When Sir Archie reached the narrow stair and the lobby, he held Elsalill before him in the same way. And she protected him better than the strongest armour, for the pikemen who were drawn up there could make no use of their weapons. Thus he came a good way up the steps, and Elsalill could feel the free air of heaven blowing about her.

But Elsalill's love for Sir Archie was changed to the most deadly hatred, and her only thought was that he was a villain and a murderer. And when she saw that her body shielded him, so that he was likely to escape, she stretched out her hand and took hold of one of the watchmen's pikes and aimed it at her heart. "Now I will serve my foster sister, so that her mission shall be fulfilled at last," thought Elsalill. And at the next step Sir Archie took up the stairs, the pike entered Elsalill's heart.

But then Sir Archie was already at the top of the stairway. And the pikemen fell back when they saw that one of them had hurt the maid. And he ran past them.

When Sir Archie came out into the market-place he heard a Scottish war cry from one of the lanes: "A rescue! A rescue! For Scotland! For Scotland!

It was Sir Philip and Sir Reginald, who had mustered the Scots and now came to relieve him.

And Sir Archie ran toward them and cried in a loud voice: "Hither to me! For Scotland! For Scotland!

As Sir Archie walked out over the ice he still held Elsalill on his arm.

Sir Philip and Sir Reginald walked beside him. They tried to tell him how they had discovered the trap laid for them and how they had succeeded in getting the heavy treasure chest away to the gallias and in collecting their countrymen; but Sir Archie paid no heed to their words. He seemed to be conversing with her he carried on his arm.

"Who is that you carry there?" asked Sir Reginald.

"It is Elsalill," answered Sir Archie. "I shall take her with me to Scotland. I will not leave her behind. Here she would never be aught but a poor fish wench."

"No, that is like enough," said Sir Reginald.

"Here none would give her clothes but of the coarsest wool," said Sir Archie, "and a narrow bed of hard planks to sleep on. But I shall spread her couch with the softest cushions, and her resting-place shall be made of marble. I shall wrap her in the costliest furs, and on her feet she shall wear jewelled shoes."

"You intend her great honour," said Sir Reginald.

"I cannot let her stay behind here," said Sir Archie, "for who among them would be mindful of such a poor creature? She would be forgotten by all ere many months were past. None would visit her abode, none would relieve her loneliness. But when once I reach home, I shall rear a stately dwelling for her. There shall her name stand graven in the hard stone, that none may forget it. There I myself shall come to her every day, and all shall be so splendidly devised that folk from far away shall come to visit her. There shall be lamps and candles burning night and day, and the sound of music and song shall make it seem a perpetual festival."

The gale blew violently in their faces as they walked over the ice. It tore Elsalill's cloak loose and made it flutter like a banner.

"Will you help me to carry Elsalill a moment," said Sir Archie, "while I wind her cloak about her?"

Sir Reginald took Elsalill in his arms, but as he did so he was so terrified that he let her slip between his hands on to the ice. "I knew not that Elsalill was dead," he said.

All night the skipper of the great gallias walked back and forth on his lofty poop. It was dark, and the gale howled around him, lashing him with sleet and rain. But the ice still lay firm and fast about the vessel, so that the skipper might just as well have slept quietly in his berth.

But he stayed up the whole night. Time after time he put his hand to his ear and listened.

It was not easy to say what he was listening for. He had all his crew on board, as well as all the passengers he was to carry over to Scotland. Every one of them lay below decks fast asleep, and there was no sound of talk to which the skipper might be listening.

As the storm came sweeping over the icebound gallias it threw itself upon the vessel, as though from old habit it would drive her through the water. And as the ship still stood fast the wind took hold of her again and again. It rattled all the little icicles that hung from her ropes and tackles, it made her timbers creak and groan. Her masts were strained and gave loud cracks, as though they would go by the board.

It was no quiet night. There was a muffled rustling in the air, as the snow came whizzing past; there was a patter and splash as the rain came pelting down.

And in the ice one crack after another opened with a noise like thunder, as though ships of war had been at sea exchanging heavy salvoes.

But to none of this was the skipper

listening.

He stayed up the whole night, until a gray dawn spread over the sky; but still he did not hear the sound he was waiting for.

At last a singing, monotonous murmur was borne upon the night air, a rocking, caressing sound as of distant music.

Then the skipper hurried across the rowers' thwarts amidships to the lofty forecastle where his crew slept. "Turn out," he called to them, "and take your oars and boat-hooks! The time is almost come when we shall be free. I hear the roar of open water. I hear the song of the free waves."

The men left sleeping and came out at once. They posted themselves along the ship's sides, while the day slowly dawned.

When at last it was light enough for them to see what changes the night had brought, they found that all the creeks and channels were open far out to sea, but in the bay where they were frozen in not a fissure could be seen in the ice, which lay firm and unbroken.

And in the channel which led out of

this bay the ice had piled itself up into a high wall. The waves in their free play outside continually cast up floating ice upon it.

In the sound between the skerries there was a swarm of sails. All the fishing-boats which had lain icebound off Marstrand were now streaming out. The sea ran high and blocks of ice still floated among the waves, but the fishermen seemed to think they had no time to wait for safe and calm water, and they had set sail. They stood in the bows of their boats and kept a sharp lookout. Small blocks of ice they fended off with an oar, but when the big ones came they put the helm over and bore away. On the high poop of the gallias the skipper stood and watched them. He could see that they had their troubles, but he saw too that one boat after another wriggled through and came out into the open sea.

And when the skipper saw the sails gliding over the blue water, he felt his disappointment so bitterly that tears came into his eyes.

But his ship lay still, and before him the wall of ice was piling up higher and higher.

The sea outside bore not only ships and boats, but sometimes small white icebergs came floating past. They were big ice-floes that had been thrown one upon another and were now sailing southward. They shone like silver in the morning sun, and now and then they showed as pink as though they had been strewed with roses.

But high up among the whistling of the wind loud cries were heard, now like singing voices, now like pealing trumpets. There was a sound of jubilation in these cries, swelling the heart of him who heard them. They came from a long flight of swans on their way from the south.

But when the skipper saw the icebergs moving southward and the swans flying to the north such longing seized him that he wrung his hands. "Woe's me, that I must lie here!" he said. "Will the ice never break up in this bay? I may lie waiting here many days yet."

Just as he said this, he saw a man come

driving on the ice. He came out of a narrow channel on the Marstrand side, and he drove as calmly on the ice as if he did not know the waves had begun once more to carry ships and boats.

As he drove under the stern of the gallias he hailed the skipper: "Ho, you there, frozen in the ice, do you lack food aboard? Will you buy my salt herring or dried ling or smoked eel?"

The skipper did not trouble to answer him. He only shook his fist at him and swore.

Then the fish hawker stepped off his load. He took a bunch of hay from the sledge and laid it in front of his horse. Then he climbed up on the deck of the gallias.

When he faced the skipper he said to him very earnestly:

"Today I have not come to sell fish. But I know that you are a God-fearing man. Therefore I have come to ask your help to find a maiden whom the Scotsmen brought out to your ship with them yesternight."

"I know naught of their bringing any

maiden with them," said the skipper. "I have heard no woman's voice aboard the ship tonight."

"I am Torarin the fish hawker," said the other; "maybe you have heard of me? It was I who supped with Herr Arne at Solberga parsonage the same night he was murdered. Since then I have had Herr Arne's foster daughter under my roof, but last night she was stolen away by his murderers, and they have surely brought her with them to your vessel."

"Are Herr Arne's murderers aboard my vessel?" asked the skipper in dismay.

"You see that I am a poor and feeble man," said Torarin. "I have a palsied arm, and therefore I am fearful of taking upon myself any bold and hazardous thing. I have known these many days who were Herr Arne's murderers, but I have not dared to bring them to justice. And because I have held my peace they have made their escape and have found occasion to carry the maiden with them. But now I have said to myself that I will have no more of my conscience in this matter. At least I will try to save the little maid."

"If Herr Arne's murderers are on board my ship, why does not the watch come out and arrest them?"

"I have begged and prayed them all this night and morning," said Torarin, "but the watch durst not come out. They say there are a hundred men-at-arms on board, and with them they durst not contend. Then I thought, in God's name I must come out here alone and beg you help me to find the maiden, for I know you to be a God-fearing man."

But the skipper paid no heed to his question of the maiden; his mind was full of the other matter. "What makes you sure that the murderers are on board?" he said.

Torarin pointed to a great oaken chest which stood between the rowers' thwarts. "I have seen that chest too often in Herr Arne's house to be mistaken," he said. "In it is Herr Arne's money, and where his money is, there you will find his murderers."

"That chest belongs to Sir Archie and

his two friends, Sir Reginald and Sir Philip,"
said the skipper.

"Ay," said Torarin, looking at him fixedly;
"that is so. It belongs to Sir Archie and
Sir Philip and Sir Reginald."

The skipper stood silent awhile and looked
this way and that. "When think you the
ice will break up in this bay?" he said
to Torarin.

"There is something strange in it this
year," said Torarin. "In this bay we have
always seen the ice break up early, for
there is a strong current. But as it shapes
now you must have a care that you be
not thrust against the land when the ice
begins to move."

"I think of naught else," said the skipper.

Again he stood silent for a while and
turned his face toward the sea. The morning sun shone high in the sky, and the
waves reflected its radiance. The liberated
vessels scudded this way and that, and the
sea birds came flying from the south with
joyous cries. The fish lay near the surface
and glittered in the sun as they leapt high
out of the water, wanton after their long

imprisonment under the ice. The gulls, which had been circling out beyond the edge of the ice, came in great flocks toward land to fish in their old waters.

The skipper could not endure this sight. "Shall I be counted the friend of murderers and evildoers?" he said. "Can I close my eyes and refuse to see why God keeps the gates of the sea barred against my vessel? Shall I be destroyed for the sake of the unrighteous who have taken refuge with me?"

And the skipper went forward and said to his men: "Now I know why we have been held back while all other ships have put to sea. It is because we have murderers and evildoers on board."

Then the skipper went to the Scottish men-at-arms, who still lay asleep in the ship's hold. "Listen," he said to them; "keep you quiet yet awhile, no matter what cries or tumult you may hear on board. We must follow God's commandment and not suffer evildoers amongst us. If you obey me I promise to bring you the chest which holds Herr Arne's money, and you shall share it among you."

But to Torarin the skipper said: "Go down to your sledge and cast your fish out on the ice. You shall have other freight anon."

Then the skipper and his men broke into the cabin where Sir Archie and his friends slept. And they threw themselves upon them to bind them while they still lay asleep.

And when the three Scotsmen tried to defend themselves, they smote them hard with their axes and handspikes, and the skipper said to them: "You are murderers and evildoers. How could you think to escape punishment? Know you not that it is for your sake God keeps all the gates of the sea closed?"

Then the three men cried aloud to their comrades, bidding them come and help them.

"You need not call to them," said the skipper. "They will not come. They have gotten Herr Arne's hoard to share amongst them, and are even now measuring out silver coin in their hats. For the sake of this money the evil deed was done, and this money has now brought retribution upon you."

And before Torarin had finished unloading the fish from his sledge, the skipper and his men came down on to the ice. They brought with them three men securely bound. They were grievously hurt and fainting from their wounds.

"God has not called on me in vain," said the skipper. "As soon as His will was clear to me, I hearkened to it."

They laid the prisoners on the sledge, and Torarin drove with them by creeks and narrow sounds where the ice still lay firm, until he came to Marstrand.

Now late in the afternoon the skipper stood on the lofty poop of his vessel and looked out to seaward. Nothing was changed around the vessel, and the wall of ice towered ever higher before her.

Then the skipper saw a long procession of people coming out to his ship. All the women of Marstrand were there, both young and old. They all wore mourning weeds, and they brought with them a group of boys who carried a bier.

When they were come to the gallias, they said to the skipper: "We are come to fetch a young maiden who is dead. Those murderers have confessed that she gave her life to hinder their escape, and now we, all the women of Marstrand, are come to bring her to our town with all the honour that is her due."

Then Elsalill was found and brought down to the ice and borne in to Marstrand; and all the women in the place wept over the young maid, who had loved an evildoer and given her life to destroy him she loved.

But even as the line of women advanced, the wind and waves broke in behind them and tore up the ice over which they had but lately passed; and when they came to Marstrand with Elsalill, all the gates of the sea stood open.